Otis
AND
THE Scarecrow

Otis

AND THE
Scarecrow

LOREN
LONG

SCHOLASTIC INC.

It was summer when the scarecrow first came to the farm where the friendly little tractor named Otis lived, back when the corn was tall and ripe.

Otis recalled how the crows had scattered at first. They wanted nothing to do with the scarecrow, which made the farmer very happy. Otis was also happy. A new friend had come to live on the farm.

But when Otis went to welcome him, the scarecrow didn't smile or say hello. He just stood there, a sour look on his face, staring at the cornfield. After a while, Otis left him alone.

When the farm animals came by to greet the scarecrow, once again he didn't smile or say hello. He just stood there, that sour look on his face, staring at the cornfield. The animals didn't know what to think. Who was this new creature?

The horse curled his lip at the scarecrow's musty smell. The ducks pointed at his

tattered clothes. The little calf and the puppy were frightened by him. Finally, the bull snarled, huffed, and turned away. And the scarecrow stood there, alone.

Summer passed, and by and by, the crows came back around. They perched, picked, and pecked at the scarecrow. Otis noticed that the scarecrow didn't shoo them away. He just stood there with that sour look on his face, staring off at the cornfield. Otis *puff*ed a soft sigh and turned to catch up with his friends.

Autumn eventually arrived. The days grew shorter and cooler. Harvest time had left the fields bare except for the plump pumpkins dotting the fields orange. Otis began pulling wagons filled with children eager to pick out a pumpkin to carve into a jack-o'-lantern. The farm looked different, but Otis loved the changing seasons, and he worked and played as hard as ever, *putt puff puttedy chuff.*

It was a splendid time on the farm for being together with family and friends.

The cool air drifting through the hills made the animals more rambunctious than ever. A simple game of follow-the-leader turned into a reckless race over the rolling hills. A game of hide-and-seek turned into a rowdy rendition of ring-around-the-rosy, the animals playfully circling Otis as he sat counting one-*putt*, two-*puff*, three-

puttedy, four-*chuff!* When Otis tuckered out from all the games, he headed up the
hill to the apple tree. His frisky friends would join him, and when they were all
sitting together, Otis would challenge everyone to a different game . . .

. . . the quiet game. The quiet game is a contest in which everyone must stay quiet and still. No sounds, no laughing, no snorting, quacking, giggling, or *puffing*. The player who stays quiet the longest wins.

Otis knew the animals loved playing any game, even one that challenged them to sit still. To start the game, he would surge his engine to get everyone's attention, take in a deep breath of air, and let out a long, soft *putt puff puttedy shhhhhh.*

Otis would sit quietly and look over the farm.

There was Mud Pond, full with the autumn rains. There were the plump pumpkins dotting the fields orange. There were the shocks of corn fodder, all in a row.

And there, still, was the scarecrow, all alone, staring sternly at
the empty cornfield.

The puppy was always the first to lose the quiet game. He just couldn't sit still!

The bull would twitch his nose, which made the little calf giggle. This made the bull chuckle with a snort. The bull's snort would amuse the ducks, and their bottoms would wiggle as they held back their giggles. The sight of the ducks' wiggling bottoms would amuse the horse so

much that he would roll on the ground, neighing with laughter. At this, the ducks would quack out loud, and soon everyone would be laughing, snorting, quacking, and giggling.

This always left Otis the winner, a big grin on his face as he sat under the apple tree with his friends.

One day, a cold rain set in. Otis and the animals ran for cover under the apple tree. They huddled together for warmth as Otis looked over the farm.

There was the overflowing Mud Pond. There were the shiny wet pumpkins and the soaked corn shocks all in a row. And there, swaying back and forth in the cold wind and rain, was the scarecrow.

Otis couldn't take his eyes off of him. He thought about how the scarecrow must feel.

Otis stood up.

He marched down the hill,
putt puff puttedy chuff,

and crossed into

the empty cornfield.

Without hesitation, Otis *chuff*ed and
*puff*ed straight up to the scarecrow.

Back under the apple tree, the animals watched intently.

Otis looked up into the painted eyes of the scarecrow and smiled. The scarecrow didn't smile back. He just stared off at the empty cornfield, as always. The two of them stood quietly in that great big field as the wind and rain battered them.

Then Otis turned his body around and backed right up
alongside the scarecrow. And with a *chuff*, he sat down
next to him.

Suddenly, the little calf and the puppy scampered down the hillside, crossed into the cornfield, and curled up right next to Otis. Gradually, the cow and horse ambled down the hillside. Before long, the ducks waddled their way down, too.

And finally, the big bull sauntered down into the field, joining the others.

Otis surged his engine to get everyone's attention, took in a deep breath of air, and let out a long, soft *putt puff puttedy shhhhhh.*

Otis and the animals sat quietly.

Until the puppy couldn't sit still another minute. The bull snorted on the calf's ears, the ducks wiggled their bottoms, and soon everyone was giggling, quacking, laughing, and even *puff*ing.

Everyone except the scarecrow, of course, who never
uttered a sound.

Yet as Otis watched, he couldn't be sure, but he thought he might have seen the scarecrow smile. Either way, Otis thought, the scarecrow didn't look so lonely anymore, surrounded by friends.

THE END

To Warren

ISBN 978-0-545-91807-7

12 11 10 9 8 7 6 5 4 3 2 1   15 16 17 18 19 20/0

Printed in the U.S.A.   08

First Scholastic printing, September 2015

Edited by Michael Green
Design by Semadar Megged
Text set Engine
The art was created in gouache and pencil.